I0726647

# The Wit And Wisdom of Plum Duff

## Hot Cross Puns

David Spencer

Ordering Information:
For orders and inquiries, please contact:
books@authorsnote360.com
www.authorsnote360.com

Printed in the United States of America

Writing a book is a journey. It needs imagination, motivation and of course passion. Publishing my books will not be realized without the support of the people around me.

I'd like to start with Emma Reading (My Wife's Mother) for all the compliments and words of encouragement she has given me. Her words served as my guide to the right direction in writing.

To my very good friends Sam Wilson and Jeff Yelton for all the support they have shown and for pushing me to work on my book.

To our family friends:

Sandy and Fred Hardy
Tim and Carol Dionne

Our family is so blessed to have a family friend like you. Always remember that you are always dear to our family.

To my Publisher Author's Note 360, I thank you for showing interest and for believing in my book. I thank the whole team for making this republication possible.

Finally, I dedicate this book to my beautiful and ever supportive wife Marilyn Spencer, the LOVE OF MY LIFE. She's been a huge fan of my books and she supported me all the way. She stood by me in sickness and in health. She's always been the source of my strength and my inspiration. Without her, I'm not sure if I'd be able to finish even a single book. To my beloved Marilyn, I thank you and I love you so much.

# "HOT CROSS" PUNCH LINES

# The History Of "Plum Duff"

In 1982, I was reading a column in the "Life/Styles" section of the Gary Post-Tribune Newspaper. The columnist, a Mr. Blaine Marz, had a fictional character that he used from time to time called, "Hashish McTavish".

My cartoon character, "Plum Duff", seemed perfect for the column, so I sent some drawings in to the paper. In a column called, ***"Reader has own concept of Hash"*** (Hashish McTavish.) Mr. Marz wrote, "Spencer, formerly Szpejnowski, sent along sketches of several other of his cartoon characters, including Crabb Apple, who might be more appropriate for the McTavish of late than the obviously more lighthearted Plum Duff. I almost wrote it, Plum Mc Duff."

Along with the drawing of the Scottish Plum smoking a pipe, Mr. Marz used a poem that I had written, entitled, *"Uncle Tony"*. Later, in November, 1983 Mr. Marz used the "Plum Duff" character in a column that included my poem, *"Starlight on Snowdrifts."*

Plum Duff was shown for a third time, when I sent in a cartoon for the Gary Post-Tribune "Future" contest. The idea was to describe how Northwest Indiana would look in the future. Plum Duff was shown next to a drawing of Steel Mill in Gary that had a big "closed" sign on it. My entry got an Honorable Mention.

Now that I have retired, I have decided to share "Plum Duff" and the others with the world. I hope that everyone will enjoy the drawings, along with the "Hot Cross Puns."

David Spencer
February, 2016

"Plum Duff" is a Scottish Plum who smokes a pipe, named after a desert found in Scotland. - He wears a Scottish hat, called a "tam-o-shanter" -

Other characters are: Prune Danish, and Crabb Apple

Oh yes, they all have:

"HOT CROSS PUNS!!"

It's the day of the INTERNATIONAL CHARIOT RACE!
The bridge is out! You have to:
**SWING LOW, SWEDE CHARIOT!!**

What "Star Wars" character had a pet insect? **LUKE FLY WALKER!**

Did you hear about the "Gourmet Bridge Builder"? He ate so
much, that he got
**TOO BIG FOR HIS BRIDGES!!**

How did they catch the "Pop-Gun" Bandit?
By the PRINTS on his POPPER!
Get it? "The *Prince* and the *Pauper*"!

TWO TERMITES ARE HAVING DINNER IN A MUSIC STORE.
WHILE EATING A PIANO LEG, ONE SAYS: "KNOW WHAT'S FOR DESERT? **CELLO**!"

Jack the Farmer is making a speech about beans: Everybody wants to hear:
**JACK AND THE BEAN-TALK!!**

Admiral Byrd says:
Why did the Cow cross the road? To get to the **UDDER SIDE!!**

The weather today will be MUGGY.
Followed by TUE-GGIE, WE-GGIE, THUR-GIE, AND FRI -GGIE!!

Everyone knows that the best bags of PEAT MOSS at the gardening store are at the bottom of the pile!
That's why you have to: **PICK A LOW PEAT!**
Get it?: "Piccolo Pete"!!

Prune Danish says:
"The speech that the King had made out of giant stone blocks was made into a huge cattle pen!
They sure put a lot of **STOCK** in his **WORDS!!**"

Oh, he married the BAKER'S DAUGHTER, but he only loved her Father's **DOUGH!**

Even though he was well - **BREAD,** he had a **LOT OF CRUST!!**

Oh, he married the Moon-Shiner's daughter, but he loves her **STILL!!**

When Jumbo, the Circus Elephant got married, his Mother-in-Law, Queenie did not lose a daughter: She gained a **TON!!**

Cleopatra of Egypt never believed ANYTHING that ANYONE told her!
That is why she was the **"QUEEN OF DE- NIAL!!"**

Old and stale coffee is made from:
**"HAS - BEANS!"**

After playing his harp at Sam the Crab's Disco, Fred the Fish said, "Oh, no! I left my **HARP** in **SAM CRAB'S DISCO!**" Get it? "I left my heart in San Francisco!"

Mr. Sam Evening married his new wife, Janet -
Now, they are: **SAM** and **JANET EVENING!**
Get it? The song "Sam enchanted evening!")

What kind of snake do you find on the windshield of your car?
car?
A "Vinda - Viper"!

The Rabbit who works at the Hospital is called: **"THE ETHER BUNNY"**

If Darth Vader had married Ella Fitgerald, then she would have been:
**ELLA - VADER!**

Do you know why the Indian Chief always wear a hat in Winter?
To keep his **WIGWAM!**
Get it? To keep his ***WIG WARM!!***

# THE WIT AND WISDOM OF PLUM DUFF

By Spencer

(CONTINUED)

What do you call a Doctor who uses a LOT of BANDAGES?
The **WIZARD** of **GAUZE!!**

Two peanuts were walking down the street, and ONE was **A-SALTED!!**

CRABB APPLE SAYS:
NOBODY CAN RAIN ON MY TIRADE!

WART BOND, THE FROG, SAYS:
WHEN TAKING YOUR LUGGAGE HOME TO YOUR
LILY PAD,
**LUG BEFORE YOU LEAP!!**

REMEMBER ONE THING:
MANY MAN SMOKE, BUT: FOO MAN CHEW

Did you hear about the movie they made about the
HAUNTED HEN -HOUSE?
It's called: **"POULTRY - GEIST!!"**

My friend the dog has no nose -
Want to know how he SMELLS? **JUST AWFUL!!**

I went to Africa, to play cards with the natives!

ZULUS?

NO, I WON!!

When it comes to building a dam, **LEAVE IT TO A BEAVER!!**

I'M BUYING SHARES IN THE STOCK MARKET! I
DECIDED TO INVEST IN: **PORK BELLIES!**

How do you listen for a train whistle, at the railroad crossing?
With your **ENGINE -EARS!!**
Get it? Your ENGINE -EERS!!

Did you hear about the ELF named JOHNNY, who made a CHAIR out of an old APPLE? Now, he is known as: **JOHNNY APPLE- SEAT!!**

Why is a KOREAN RACE HORSE like a FISH DISH?
***FILLY* OF *SEOUL!!***

Did you hear about the IRISH LAWN - CHAIR SALESMAN?
His name was: PATTY O' FURNITURE!
Get it? **"PATIO - FURNITURE!!"**

Why is getting up in the morning like a PIG'S TAIL? It's **TWIRLY!**
Get it? ***TOO EARLY: "T'WIRLY"!!***

The Ram broke up with his girlfriend. He says, "There'll never be another **EWE!!**"

I do all my washing in TIDE!
IT'S TOO *COLD*, **OUT - TIDE!!**

I planted a lot of GRASS SEED in back of my garage, by the trash cans! HOW GREEN WAS MY **ALLEY!** What? You never saw the old movie, "HOW GREEN WAS MY VALLEY"?

Did you hear about the Irish Laundry Lady? Her name was:
**BEADS O' BLEACH!**

INTRODUCING:
WILD BILL **HICCUP,** THE SPONGE!

There they are!
The NORSE and the SOUSE!!

They say that Crabb Apple was wonderful to the ARMY, but: ROTTEN TO THE **CORPS!**
Get it? Rotten to the CORE!!

Why is a PEASANT'S WRISTWATCH better than the Village Clock?
Because: There's NO TIME LIKE THE **PEASANT**!
(No time like the PRESENT, get it?)

SEE YOU IN THE FUNNY PAPERS!!

CAST OF SUPPORTING CHARACTERS:
WART BOND THE FROG, ADMIRAL BYRD, JUMBO,
"ETHER" BUNNY, A. NONNY. MOUSE, RATZ-PUTIN

www.ingramcontent.com/pod-product-compliance
Lightning Source LLC
Chambersburg PA
CBHW042034180726
48295CB00001B/13